NICKELODEON

SpongeBob™
squarepants

JOKE
BOOK

Stephen Hillenburg

Based on the TV series *SpongeBob SquarePants*®
created by Stephen Hillenburg as seen on Nickelodeon®

SIMON SPOTLIGHT

An imprint of Simon & Schuster Children's Publishing Division
1230 Avenue of the Americas, New York, New York 10020

Manufactured in the United States of America

First Edition
6 8 10 9 7 5

ISBN 0-689-84017-9

NICKELODEON

SpongeBob™
squarepants

Joke
Book

BY DAVID LEWMAN

Simon Spotlight/Nickelodeon

New York   London   Toronto   Sydney   Singapore

What does Patrick's best friend take before he goes to bed?

A sponge bath.

How did Squidward feel when he found an electric eel in his clarinet?

He was shocked.

Who's yellow and dances in an undersea barn?

SpongeBob SquareDance.

What does Patrick's best
friend keep in his closet?
SpongeBob's spare pants.

What happened when SpongeBob played
checkers against Squidward?
He beat him fair and square.

Why can you trust SpongeBob?
He always gives you a square deal.

What does SpongeBob eat
three times a day?
A square meal.

Sandy: Knock, knock.

SpongeBob: Who's there?

Sandy: Sweat.

SpongeBob: Sweat who?

Sandy: 'S wet down here, isn't it?

Patrick: Why did the fish stay home from school?

Mrs. Puff: She was feeling a little under the water.

Squidward: Why does SpongeBob get in so much trouble?

Mr. Krabs: Because he's always in deep water.

Where does SpongeBob sleep?
In a water bed.

SpongeBob: Knock, knock.
Squidward: Who's there?
SpongeBob: Water.
Squidward: Water who?
SpongeBob: What're you doin',
Squidward?

SpongeBob: Were you a
happy baby, Patrick?
Patrick: Yes, because I
knew someday
I'd be a star.

Pearl: What kind of
star is Patrick?
Squidward: The kind
that's not very bright.

What do you get
when you cross a
squid and a pig?

An oinktopus.

What do you get
when you cross a
squid and a parrot?

A squawktopus.

Who robs banks
and shoots ink?
Billy the Squid.

Are shellfish warm?
No, they're clammy.

What would Sandy be if she got her picture in a magazine?
A cover squirrel.

What did SpongeBob say
after he fell in the dough?
"I'm bready!"

Who cleans the rooms at
Bikini Bottom's hotel?
Mer-maids.

What has a girl's head, a fish's
tail, and speaks very softly?
A murmurmaid.

What has a cat's head and
a fish's tail?
A purrmaid.

What has two seats,
and sticks to underwater
rocks?
A barnacle built for two.

What do his friends sing on SpongeBob's birthday?

"For he's a jolly good yellow!"

How does SpongeBob learn about new parts of the ocean?

He lets it all soak in.

Why did the seal always get average grades?

He was a C Lion.

What's big and gray and lives underwater?

An eelephant.

How did Patrick do on his bubble test?

He blew it.

Who's the best dressed creature in the ocean?

The swordfish—he always looks sharp!

What do you get when you cross a fish and a grizzly?
A bearacuda.

Which fish is the cheesiest?
The barragouda.

Which fish is
the smelliest?
The stink ray.

Why did SpongeBob
chase the stinging fish?
He wanted to
catch some rays.

Why did the stingray
speak to the diver?

He wanted to have
a manta-man talk.

Why did the scary fish always swim by himself?
He wanted to be a lone shark.

What do you get when you cross a shellfish and a rabbit?
The Oyster Bunny.

What do you get when you cross a scary fish with an anteater?
An aardshark.

How did the wave feel about hitting the beach?
He was fit to be tide.

Who got to the beach first, the big wave or the little wave?
In the end, they were tide.

27

Which sea creature makes
the best sandwiches?
The peanut-butter-and-jellyfish.

Where do fish like to
go on vacation?
Finland.

Which book is every fish's favorite?
Huckleberry Fin.

Which whale is
the saddest?
The blue whale.

What will happen to Plankton if
he breaks the law?
He'll be thrown
in whale.

Why does Patrick think octopuses are sweet? He heard they're covered with suckers.

What do you call an underwater sheep? A scubaaaaaa diver.

How did Sandy feel when she first reached Bikini Bottom? She was floored.

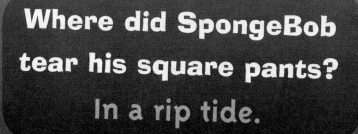

Where did SpongeBob tear his square pants?

In a rip tide.

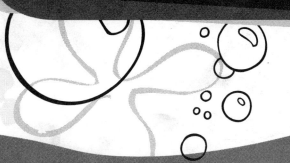

What's every porpoise's favorite musical?

Guys and Dolphins.

SpongeBob: Knock, knock.

Squidward: Who's there?

SpongeBob: Conch.

Squidward: Conch who?

SpongeBob: Conch you open this door?

What do you use to catch starfish?

A film reel.

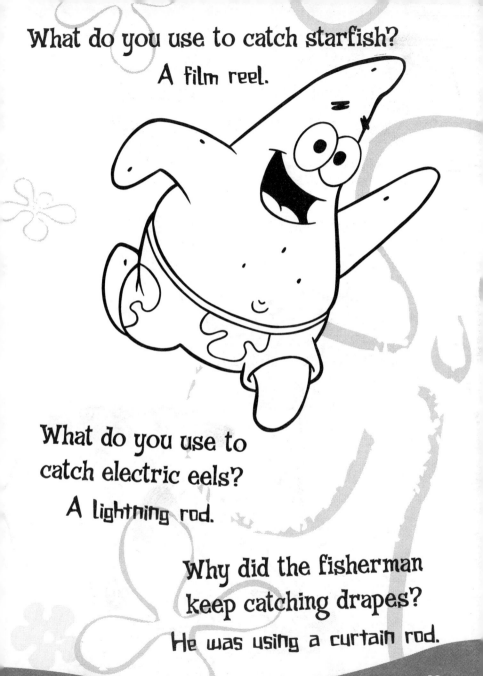

What do you use to
catch electric eels?

A lightning rod.

Why did the fisherman
keep catching drapes?

He was using a curtain rod.

Why did the ocean flood the stadium?
It was doing the wave!

Why did Plankton
punch the sand?
He wanted to hit
the beach.

What does SpongeBob
use to write home
from the beach?
Sandpaper.

SpongeBob and Patrick: Knock, knock.

Squidward: Who's there?

SpongeBob and Patrick: Seaweed.

Squidward: Seaweed who?

SpongeBob and Patrick: See, we'd come in if you'd open the door.

Where did the seaweed
find a job?
In the
"Kelp Wanted" ads.

Why did SpongeBob salute his boss?
He wanted to hail a crab.

How did the jury find the fish?
Gill-ty.

What happened when
SpongeBob rode on his pet snail?
He got Gary-ied away.

What's Gary like first
thing in the morning?
A little sluggish.

Which fish is
the funniest?
The cartoona.

What game do fish
love to play?
Salmon Says.

How did SpongeBob get across the beach so quickly?

He took a shore-cut.

How do you stop a *fish* stampede?

Head 'em off at the bass.

SpongeBob and Patrick: Knock, knock.

Squidward: Who's there?

SpongeBob and Patrick: Porous.

Squidward: Porous who?

SpongeBob and Patrick: Pour us something to drink—we're thirsty!

When SpongeBob's neighbor talks, what comes out of his mouth?

Squid words.

What does Patrick listen to in his home?

Rock music.

What do you use to cut the ocean?

A seasaw.

What do you get when you cross an ape and a crustacean?

A shrimpanzee.

Why did the coral stand on his head? He wanted to turn over a new reef.

Why don't little fish sleep at night? They're afraid of the shark.

Which squid is the friendliest?
The cuddlefish.

Why did the cantaloupe
jump in the ocean?
It wanted to be a
watermelon.

When is SpongeBob like a bell?
When he's wrung out.

What did the patty
do when it saw
SpongeBob's new
spatula?
It flipped.

SpongeBob: Can't you say anything nice about Patrick?

Squidward: He has his points.

Which part of a boat is the grouchiest?

The stern.

Which part of a boat is the most polite?

The bow.

How do you catch cyberfish?

With an **Internet**.

Which fish hates to be alone?

The grouper.

Which fish can slide across ice?

The skate.

SpongeBob: Knock, knock.

Squidward: Who's there?

SpongeBob: Saul.

Squidward: Saul who?

SpongeBob: Saltwater's the best—got any?

What happened when SpongeBob invited too many people onto his boat?
He went a little overboard.

Why did the ocean take the afternoon off?
He wanted to play gulf.

Which fish finds the best bargains?
The sale-fish